Sticking

Mrs. Becker's class the twins up the zoo path. "Come on, we have to catch up," Elizabeth warned.

But Jessica wouldn't move. "I want to see the monkeys. I *don't* want to see the snakes."

Todd and Winston were running back toward them. "Where are you going?" Todd asked.

"I'm going to see the monkeys," Jessica stated.

Elizabeth's stomach flip-flopped. "Jess! Please!"

"N-O spells no. And you have to stay, Liz. We're buddies."

"We're buddies, too," Winston said. He looked at Todd. "Do you want to stay with them?"

Todd shrugged his shoulders. "I guess so. Besides, the others are gone," he pointed out.

Elizabeth gulped. They were on their own!

SWEET VALLEY KIDS

JESSICA'S ZOO ADVENTURE

Written by
Molly Mia Stewart

Created by
FRANCINE PASCAL

Illustrated by
Ying-Hwa Hu

A BANTAM SKYLARK BOOK®
NEW YORK • TORONTO • LONDON • SYDNEY • AUCKLAND

To Sara Anne Weiss

RL 2, 005–008

JESSICA'S ZOO ADVENTURE
A Bantam Skylark Book / June 1990

*Sweet Valley High® and Sweet Valley Kids are
trademarks of Francine Pascal*

Conceived by Francine Pascal

*Produced by Daniel Weiss Associates, Inc.
33 West 17th Street
New York, NY 10011*

Cover art by Susan Tang

*Skylark Books is a registered trademark of Bantam Books, a division of
Bantam Doubleday Dell Publishing Group, Inc.*

ISBN 0-553-15802-3

Published simultaneously in the United States and Canada

*Bantam Books are published by Bantam Books, a division of Bantam Double-
day Dell Publishing Group, Inc. Its trademark, consisting of the words
"Bantam Books" and the portrayal of a rooster, is Registered in U.S. Patent
and Trademark Office and in other countries. Marca Registrada. Bantam
Books, 666 Fifth Avenue, New York, New York 10103.*

PRINTED IN THE UNITED STATES OF AMERICA

CWO   0 9 8 7 6 5 4 3

CHAPTER 1

Zoo News

"I can't wait!" Elizabeth Wakefield said, hopping up and down in front of the refrigerator. "I love the zoo!"

"Are you a kangaroo?" asked her twin sister, Jessica. She began to hop up and down, too, and then she bumped into Elizabeth. They both started giggling.

Elizabeth and Jessica sounded just the same when they laughed, and they looked just the same, too. Both girls had long blond hair with bangs and bright blue-green eyes.

When they wore matching outfits to school, it was impossible to tell them apart.

Because they looked exactly alike on the outside, many people thought Elizabeth and Jessica were exactly alike on the inside. But each girl had her own special personality. Elizabeth liked reading and making up stories, and she liked playing adventure games outside. Jessica wasn't happy unless she had someone to talk to. She thought school was for whispering in class, and her favorite part of the day was recess.

Those differences weren't really important, though, because they were best friends. Elizabeth and Jessica did almost everything together. They shared a bedroom, they wore the same clothing, and they even shared gum sometimes!

"What are you two monkeys giggling

about?" asked Mr. Wakefield as he walked into the kitchen with the newspaper in his hand.

"We're not monkeys, we're kangaroos!" Elizabeth told him. She started hopping again.

Their older brother, Steven, was already at the breakfast table. "You look like lizards," he said.

Jessica stuck her tongue out at him. "You're just jealous because we're going to the zoo for our class trip," she said. "And Mom's going with us, too."

Steven looked up at the ceiling. "Big deal."

"Here's another article about the zoo in the newspaper," Mr. Wakefield said.

"Where?" Elizabeth asked. She ran to his side to look. "What does it say?"

Her father ruffled her hair. "You read it to me."

"OK." Elizabeth stood at her place at the table and read the headline out loud: "Birth of Baby Animals Adds to Zoo Family." Elizabeth grinned. "I bet they're really cute!"

Jessica began sipping her juice without picking up the glass. "What kind of baby animals?" she wanted to know.

Elizabeth read the paragraph. "It says a baby bear cub *and* a tiger cub were born yesterday!"

"I want to see the tiger cub!" Jessica gasped. "I bet it's like a big kitten!"

The newspaper had had articles on all the new zoo babies for several weeks. Elizabeth knew there were many animals to see, but the baby animals would be the best part about going to the zoo!

Elizabeth sat down and poured cereal into her bowl. "I want to see all the animals, but I want to see the monkeys most of all."

"Me, too!" Jessica agreed loudly.

"What's all the excitement about?" Mrs. Wakefield asked as she walked into the kitchen.

Jessica jumped up. "Mom! Mom! Since you're going to be class mother, can we see the monkeys first?"

Mrs. Wakefield laughed. "Just because I'm coming along doesn't mean you get to pick what the class sees," she said.

"But will we get to see everything?" Elizabeth asked hopefully.

"If we have time," Mrs. Wakefield said.

Jessica wiggled around in her seat. "I can't wait! Hurry, Liz, we have to leave soon."

"You have lots of time. Remember, you're

6

not taking the school bus today," Mrs. Wakefield reminded them. "I'm driving us to school."

Elizabeth was so excited she could hardly wait to finish her cereal. The whole day was going to be special. Even driving to school in the car with their mother would be fun. She let out a deep breath.

"What's wrong, Elizabeth?" Mr. Wakefield asked.

"Nothing, Dad. I'm just excited!" she answered as she pushed her chair closer to her sister. "Remember when we went to the zoo last year and saw those huge elephants?"

Jessica nodded, and her blue-green eyes widened. "And they took peanuts out of our hands! That was great!"

"I hope we get to do that again," Elizabeth said.

"I hope we get to do *everything!*" Jessica shouted.

Elizabeth laughed. It was going to be their best field trip ever!

CHAPTER 2

Bossy Jessica

Jessica led the way into Mrs. Becker's second-grade classroom. "You can sit in my seat, Mom," she said proudly, after Mrs. Wakefield had said hello to their teacher.

"Thank you, Jessica," Mrs. Wakefield said.

Lila Fowler, who was Jessica's best friend after Elizabeth, walked into the classroom. "Hi, Mrs. Wakefield!" she called out.

"My mother is going with us!" Jessica told her.

Lila nodded. "I know. You've been telling us that since last week."

Jessica pretended not to hear her. She looked at her sister. "If we use the Buddy System today, let's be buddies."

"OK," Elizabeth agreed.

All of their classmates were laughing and talking and telling each other what their favorite animals were. Winston Egbert was saving a banana for a snack, but he pretended to eat it the way a gorilla would.

Jessica looked all around the room with a big smile on her face. She was happy that her mother was there. It made her stand out from the others.

"Class," Mrs. Becker said loudly over the excited chatter "I'm very happy you all got permission to come. I'll take attendance on the bus. Right now I want each of you to choose a buddy for the day." She waited as everyone shuffled around the room to pair off. "Now do you all have a buddy?"

"YES!" everyone shouted.

Mrs. Becker nodded. "Fine. Now, let's line up!"

The room became as noisy as a zoo again. Elizabeth and Jessica were toward the back of the line. In front of them, Charlie Cashman and Jerry McAllister were teasing Lois Waller. Lois started to sniffle as they walked out into the hall.

"I'll tell my mother," Jessica whispered to Charlie importantly. "You'd better watch out or you'll get in trouble."

Charlie and Jerry pretended to be afraid. "Please don't tell on us!" Charlie whimpered. Then he and Jerry poked each other in the ribs and laughed.

"They're just jealous," Jessica told Elizabeth.

"Of what?" Elizabeth asked in surprise.

Jessica gave her sister a know-it-all look. "Because Mom is class mother." Mrs. Wakefield was walking up front with Mrs. Becker. "Let's walk with Mom," Jessica said, pulling Elizabeth's hand.

"Jessica! Wait!" Elizabeth said.

"Hey, no fair cutting!" Caroline Pearce said in a loud voice. Elizabeth cut in next to Jessica, looking sorry.

"We're not cutting," Jessica snapped at Caroline.

Mrs. Wakefield turned around. "Jessica, weren't you and Elizabeth near the end of the line?"

Jessica's cheeks got red. "But . . ."

"We wanted to walk with you," Elizabeth explained.

"I think you should go back to where you were," their mother said in a no-nonsense voice.

Jessica stopped walking so that everyone had to zigzag around her. When Charlie and Jerry went by, she took her old place. Elizabeth joined the line next to her again.

"Mom was mean," Jessica said grumpily.

"But you shouldn't have cut," Elizabeth whispered.

"But now we won't get good seats on the bus," Jessica grumbled. "Mom should have given us first choice. It's not fair." Jessica was especially angry that her mother had scolded her in front of the whole class.

Once everyone was on the bus, Mrs.

Becker began to take attendance. While she was calling off names, Jessica leaned close to Elizabeth. "Let's see if we can trade seats with Amy and Eva," she whispered.

"Why?" Elizabeth asked.

"Because they have better seats," Jessica explained. She got up and skipped to the front where Amy and Eva sat. "Elizabeth and I should get to have your seats," she told them.

Amy blinked. "How come?"

Before Jessica could answer, Mrs. Wakefield tapped her on the shoulder and gave her a firm look. Jessica knew that she had to go back. Pouting, she dragged her feet back to where her sister sat.

"Don't be so grouchy," Elizabeth said with a smile.

Jessica slumped in her seat, but then she

15

grinned anyway. She couldn't stay angry when they were going to the zoo.

"Hey, Elizabeth," Todd Wilkins said, leaning over their seat. "Do you want to see the s-s-snakes?" He made his arm slither across her head.

"Quit it!" Elizabeth giggled.

Jessica made a face. "We're not seeing the snakes," she said.

"Says who?" Todd asked.

Jessica smiled. "Says me."

CHAPTER 3

It's Not Fair!

"Attention, everyone!" Mrs. Becker called while the class filed through the front gate of the zoo. "Mr. Ericson is the zookeeper, and he wants to tell us something."

Elizabeth stared at Mr. Ericson. He was very tall, and his cotton safari jacket had many pockets all over it. She wondered if he had helped to bring any of the animals to the zoo.

"I have an announcement for you," he began. "One of our young chimps is missing, and we've had to shut the monkey house for today."

"Oh, no," Jessica said.

"Missing?" Elizabeth gasped.

"That's right," Mr. Ericson said. "She's only four months old. She probably got scared and is hiding somewhere on the zoo grounds."

"Poor little chimp," Ellen Riteman said.

Jessica pouted. "That's not fair. I wanted to see the monkeys!"

"Well, everything else is open," Mrs. Becker pointed out. "And the first stop is the Feeding Zoo."

"Hooray!" everyone yelled.

Elizabeth held Jessica's hand as she looked at the zoo buildings and cages. There were lots of birds flying around, and squirrels running between the trees. It was very pretty. But Elizabeth thought the little chimp must be scared to be lost.

"I can't wait to feed the baby goats," Jessica said.

Elizabeth perked up. "Me, too! It'll be so much fun."

"This Way to the Feeding Zoo" said a large sign. Soon the class came to a fenced-in area where baby goats, piglets, fawns, and lambs all scampered around. "Look!" Lila giggled. "Aren't they cute?"

Even the boys looked excited. A woman in a zoo uniform handed out bottles of milk for them to feed the babies with. Elizabeth and Jessica each got one. As soon as Elizabeth went in the gate, she was surrounded by hungry babies!

"Hey," she laughed, holding her bottle out.

"One at a time!" All the animals had tiny hooves and big eyes.

"They're all so little," Jessica said, trying to hold her bottle still. A baby goat gently butted into her with its head and she dropped her plastic bottle. The milk spilled out onto the ground. "Mom!" Jessica shouted. "I need another bottle!"

Mrs. Wakefield walked over. "What happened to the one you had?" she asked.

"It fell," Jessica explained. She pointed to the ground. "Can I have another?"

"I'm sorry, Jessica. You get only one," her mother said.

Elizabeth could tell her sister was angry. "Here," she said, holding out her bottle. "You can use mine."

But Jessica turned away. "Mom could get me another one if she wanted to."

Elizabeth felt sorry for her twin. All of the other kids were handing back their empty bottles, and everyone was laughing and chattering. Everyone except Jessica.

"What are we going to see next?" Ken Matthews asked when they were back on the path again. They were such a big group that all the other visitors had to wait for them to pass. "Can we see the snakes?"

Jessica shot her hand up. "I don't want to see the snakes!" she called out. She looked at Mrs. Wakefield with a confident smile. "We don't have to see the snakes, right, Mom?"

"Jessica, we'll do what interests your classmates most," Mrs. Wakefield said. "Remember your manners."

Jessica's cheeks turned bright pink. She

pushed to the back of the group as they started walking. Elizabeth followed her.

"What's wrong?" Elizabeth asked.

"Mom keeps scolding me in front of everyone!" Jessica complained. She looked like she was about to cry. "I'm *so* mad at her!"

Elizabeth didn't like to see her sister unhappy. "Don't be mad at Mom," she said. "Let's just have fun."

Jessica crossed her arms and stopped walking. "I want to see the monkeys," she said, sulking.

"But we can't," Elizabeth said. She looked at the rest of the group. The class was walking on ahead of the twins up the path, and they turned a corner while Elizabeth watched. "Come on, we have to catch up," she warned.

But Jessica wouldn't move. "I want to see the monkeys. I *don't* want to see the snakes and Mom can't make me."

"Jessica!" Elizabeth tugged her sister's arm. "Come on! They're going without us!"

"Hey," a voice called. "You guys!"

Elizabeth and Jessica turned around. Todd and Winston were running back toward them. "Where are you going?" Todd asked curiously.

"I'm going to see the monkeys," Jessica stated.

Elizabeth's stomach flip-flopped. "Jess! Please!"

"Nope." Jessica folded her arms again and shook her head. "N-O spells no. And you have to stay, Liz. We're buddies."

"We're buddies, too," Winston said. He

looked at Todd. "Do you want to stay with them?"

Todd put his hands in his pockets and shrugged his shoulders. "I guess so. Besides, the others are gone," he pointed out.

Elizabeth gulped. They were on their own!

CHAPTER 4

Adventure!

"I'm going to the monkey house now," Jessica announced.

"Hey, look out!" Winston said suddenly. "Your bracelet is coming off!"

"Oh!" Jessica grabbed the beaded bracelet on her wrist. It was her name bracelet. Elizabeth had one just like it. The clasp on Jessica's bracelet was loose.

"Put it in your pocket," Elizabeth suggested.

"I don't want to. I want to wear it," Jessica said, fastening the clasp as best she could. "OK. Come on. Let's see the monkeys."

Todd pointed to a path on the left. "The monkey house is that way," he said. "I've been here a million times."

"No way!" Winston pointed to the right with a know-it-all look. "It's that way."

Elizabeth pointed to a sign behind them and giggled. "You're both wrong. It's that way."

Both of the boys looked embarrassed. Jessica laughed, too. "OK," she said, following the sign. "Let's go."

"This is like an adventure," Todd said. "We're explorers!"

"Hey, that's right," Elizabeth said. "Let's pretend we're in the jungle and there are wild alligators."

"And we can only walk on the path," Winston added. "If someone steps off, they get eaten by alligators."

Jessica thought they were being silly. "Come on," she said impatiently. "Let's just go!"

They were all very careful to stay on the path, even though the boys tried to push each other off. Winston's banana was getting a little bit crushed, but he said it would still taste good.

In just a few minutes, the group found the large, brick monkey house. The main door was closed. Jessica peeked over her shoulder. "Let's see if it's locked," she whispered.

She tiptoed to the door and tugged on the handle. No luck. She tried pushing the door but it still wouldn't budge.

"The sign says 'Closed,'" Elizabeth pointed out sadly.

Jessica frowned. "Maybe there's another door."

Winston and Todd both shrugged. "Could be," Todd said.

As quiet as leopards in the jungle, they tip-toed single file around the corner of the monkey house.

"Look in here," Elizabeth said. She was leaning over a stone wall.

Jessica and the boys came up close to see what she had found. On the other side of the wall was a deep pit, a bare tree, some caves, and a pool of water. It was all connected to the back of the monkey house, but no monkeys were outside.

"What's that?" Winston said. He pointed to one of the caves. "It looks like a giant, hairy leg!"

"Maybe the gorillas are in there," Elizabeth said.

"Of course," Jessica agreed. "I wish that one would wake up so we could see it."

"We could throw in Winston's banana," Todd suggested. He pretended he was going to take it out of Winston's pocket.

Winston grabbed the banana. "Why don't we throw *you* in?"

"Come on," Jessica said, heading for the side door. "Let's see if we can get in here."

But that door was locked, too, and there were no other entrances.

"We'd better forget it," Elizabeth said. "Let's go back and feed the baby animals again."

Jessica leaned against the door and folded her arms. "I don't want to," she said grumpily.

Todd and Winston were making gorilla noises and scratching their armpits to wake up the sleeping gorilla. Jessica thought the boys were dumb. She wished she could find a way to see the monkeys.

"Look at them," Elizabeth piped up.

She was pointing to a clump of trees along the pathway. Three uniformed zoo workers were looking up the trunk of one tree into the leaves. Then they went to another tree and did the same thing.

"That looks pretty weird," Winston said, laughing.

Elizabeth's eyes opened wide. "I know what they're doing," she said. "They're looking for the missing chimp!"

Jessica looked again. "You're right!"

"Wouldn't it be fun if we found the chimp?" Todd said. Everyone was very quiet. Then they all nodded at the same time.

"Let's start looking!" Jessica whispered.

CHAPTER 5

The Search is On

"Now we're on a treasure hunt!" Elizabeth said.

Todd looked serious. "Let's look in the places a chimp would hide. But where would that be?"

"I know," Jessica said. "We'll think like chimpanzees."

"That's easy for Win," Todd said with a grin. Winston started his chimpanzee act again.

Elizabeth laughed, too. "Come on, let's really try to find the chimp."

"We'd be heroes!" Jessica said. "Maybe we'd even get medals."

"I'm looking over here!" Winston yelled, running back to the gorilla pit.

"*I* was going to look over there!" Jessica said angrily. She chased after him.

Elizabeth looked at Todd. "What do you think?"

"Maybe . . ." Todd shrugged. "I don't know. Maybe it would look for food."

"Good idea," Elizabeth said. She looked down the path, and saw a squirrel sniffing at a garbage can. "Let's look in the garbage cans!" she said excitedly. "There could be leftovers inside them."

She and Todd raced to the nearest can. In it were smelly lunch bags and empty bottles, but no lost chimp.

"Did you find it?" Winston asked, running

up with Jessica. Jessica held her nose and looked into the can.

"Not in this one," Elizabeth said. "But we should look in all the garbage cans we see."

The group hurried down the pathway. Every time they found a garbage can, they looked inside. But the runaway chimp wasn't in any of them. They noticed a few more zoo workers who were looking for the chimpanzee, too.

"Maybe it went into the bathrooms," Jessica suggested when they stopped by a building with doors marked "Men" and "Women" on the outside. "I wonder which one it would go in," she added in a puzzled voice.

"It's a girl chimpanzee," Todd reminded them. "That's what Mr. Ericson the zookeeper said."

Elizabeth started laughing. "But she wouldn't know it was the girls' room or the boys' room!"

Jessica grinned. "You're right." She pointed down a pathway. "Let's look over there."

The path turned a corner and they came to a sign that said No Entry: Construction Area.

"I'm looking in here," Jessica told the others. She walked past the sign and stepped over a board.

"Jessica!" Elizabeth gasped. "You're not supposed to walk over there!"

"Right," Winston agreed. "You could get in trouble."

Jessica turned around and frowned at them. "The little chimp doesn't know this area is off limits. She could be in here. If I find her I won't be in trouble."

Elizabeth realized they would all be in big trouble, no matter what. She knew her mother was probably very worried about them. They had made a big mistake in leaving the group.

"Everybody," Elizabeth said nervously. "I think we should go back. We should try to find the others. They're probably looking for *us* right now."

"Maybe you're right," Todd mumbled.

Winston scraped the ground with his sneaker. "Yeah."

"OK," Jessica said. She let out a sigh. "Let's go back."

They began to walk back down the path, but Elizabeth wasn't sure which way they should go. It made her feel a little scared. Jessica and Todd and Winston must have felt the same way, because they were all very quiet.

Then Jessica stopped. "Oh, no!" she wailed. "My bracelet is gone!"

Elizabeth's eyes widened. "Where did you lose it?"

Instead of answering, Jessica started to cry. "We have to look for it!"

"Do we have to?" Winston said.

Todd made a face. "Can't you get another one?"

"No!" Jessica sobbed. "It was special!"

Elizabeth felt terrible. It was as if she had lost her own name bracelet. She took Jessica's hand. "We'll find it," she said. "I promise."

CHAPTER 6

What's That Noise?

The four friends hurried back along the pathways, looking down at the ground. Jessica kept sniffling and wiping her eyes. "I'll never find it," she said gloomily.

"Yes, we will," Elizabeth said reassuringly.

But Elizabeth was starting to think that the whole field trip was spoiled. Instead of having fun, they were all upset. They weren't even seeing very many animals! And she was afraid they were all going to be in big trouble once they found their mother and the class.

"Look!" Winston yelled. He bent down.

Jessica rushed to his side. "Did you find it?"

Winston stood up with a piece of yellow string in his fingers. "Oops. I made a mistake," he said. "Sorry."

Jessica's chin trembled. "We have to find it!"

"Let's go down this path," Todd said, pointing. "We were here before."

Elizabeth was getting confused. All of the paths looked the same. "Are you sure we went this way?" she asked.

"Positive," Todd said. He led the way.

"Look!" Jessica added. "There's that construction place." She ran on ahead.

Elizabeth fell behind the others as she searched the ground on either side of the path. When she caught up, Todd, Winston, and Jessica were on the other side of the "No Entry" sign.

"Be careful. Remember, we're not supposed to be here!" she warned.

"But I went this far before," Jessica said. "My bracelet could have fallen here."

Elizabeth didn't like breaking the rules, but it was important to find Jessica's bracelet. She made a face as she walked past the sign.

"I'm starving," Winston complained. He kicked over a piece of wood. "What if we miss lunch?"

Todd had a wristwatch on. "It's twelve o'clock," he said.

"I'm tired of looking," Winston said, sitting down on a big pipe. "I want to have lunch."

"Me, too," Todd agreed. He sat down next to Winston.

"No fair!" Jessica cried. "You have to help me. You have to keep looking."

Elizabeth spoke up. "I think we should

41

find Mom and the class. Maybe someone already found your bracelet."

Jessica's forehead wrinkled up angrily. Then she blinked and stopped frowning. "Shh!" she said suddenly.

The others looked at her in surprise. "What?" Winston asked.

"I said *shh!* I heard a noise!" Jessica told them.

Elizabeth and the boys were quiet. Jessica began to look all around.

"I think it came from in here," she said, walking over to one end of a large water pipe. She knelt down and peeked inside.

"Oh my gosh!" she gasped. Her blue-green eyes opened wide.

"Did you find it?" Elizabeth called. She hoped Jessica had found her bracelet. Then they could go find the rest of the class.

"Come quickly!" Jessica called excitedly.

They all crowded around Jessica at the end of the pipe.

"How did your bracelet get in here?" Elizabeth asked. She looked inside.

A tiny, frightened face was staring back at her.

"It's the chimp!" Elizabeth whispered. "You found her!"

"Wow!" Todd said.

Winston wiggled his finger at the chimp. "Come on, girl," he said. He reached inside the pipe. The chimp made a frightened sound and backed up. She was trembling.

"You're scaring her!" Jessica said angrily. "Don't try to grab her."

Elizabeth sat back on her heels and looked at the others. "What should we do?" she asked them.

"She doesn't want to come out," Todd said.

Jessica and Winston peered inside the pipe. "Come here, chimpy!" Jessica said in a soothing voice.

"Maybe we should find someone who works at the zoo," Elizabeth said. "They would know how to get her out."

"Someone should stay here, too," Jessica added. She looked excited and serious at the same time. "To make sure the chimp doesn't run away."

"I'll go," Todd said. He looked at Elizabeth. "Do you want to come with me?"

Elizabeth nodded. "Sure."

"And Jess and I will stay here," Winston said.

"Come on," Todd said.

Elizabeth took another peek at the chimp. She was huddled inside the pipe, looking scared. Elizabeth thought it was wonderful that they had found her. "OK, little chimp," Elizabeth whispered. "We'll get someone to help."

Then she stood up and looked at Todd. "Let's go!"

CHAPTER 7

Banana to the Rescue

Jessica watched Elizabeth and Todd run back down the pathway. Then she knelt beside the opening of the pipe. The frightened chimp stared back at her with big brown eyes.

"This is so great," Winston said happily. "Wait till the others hear how you found the chimp!"

Jessica smiled. "I'll be a hero," she told Winston. "And I'll tell everyone you helped." She thought that was very generous of her.

"Thanks," Winston said proudly. "I wonder how we can make her come out," he said.

"I don't know," Jessica replied. She peeked in at the chimp again. "I wish we had candy or—" She stopped talking and stared at Winston. "Give me your banana!"

Winston held the banana close to his body. "I was going to eat it," he said.

"Come on, please?" Jessica said. "If we hold it out to the chimp, she might come and get it!"

"Well . . . OK," Winston agreed. "But I get to hold it."

Jessica frowned. "I found her, so I should get to hold the banana," she said.

"But it's my banana!" Winston said stubbornly.

Jessica knew Winston could be just as stubborn as she was. "Then we'll both hold it, OK?" she said.

"OK." Winston knelt next to her and took

47

the banana out of his jacket pocket. The banana was almost black, and it smelled like a whole bunch of bananas instead of just one. The chimp started sniffing the air.

"Look," Jessica whispered. "She can already smell it."

Winston peeled the banana halfway and broke off the top.

"I get to hold the end with the peel," Jessica said quickly. "I don't want to touch the mushy part."

Winston shrugged. "I don't care. It's just banana. I'm not afraid of it."

"I'm not *afraid* of the banana," Jessica yelled. "I just don't want to get all messy!"

While they were arguing, the chimp came a step closer. Jessica and Winston both became very quiet. The chimp was now almost close enough for them to touch her.

"Come here," Jessica whispered.

Very slowly, the chimp took another step toward Jessica. She used her hands to pull herself along. Jessica could see the brown hair around her face and her long, skinny fingers. She almost looked like a small, hairy child!

"Come on," Jessica said softly. She held her section of the banana out as far as she could reach.

The chimp stared at the banana, and then reached out one hand to take it.

"Don't let go," Winston whispered.

Jessica nodded. She moved backward, so the chimp had to come even closer. Now the chimp was at the opening of the pipe. Jessica quickly peeled her half of the banana and put it down in front of her. In an instant, the little chimpanzee had put the piece into her mouth. She looked at the other piece of banana in Winston's hand.

"What if she runs away after you give her that one?" Jessica asked nervously. "Then we won't have anything else to give her."

Winston shook his head. "I don't know."

"I don't know either," Jessica said. Then she saw the chimp reaching out her hand. "Look out!"

Before Winston could pull his hand back, the chimp had eaten the other piece of the banana.

"Jessica!" Elizabeth called. "We're back!"

Jessica turned around and put one finger to her lips. "Don't scare the chimp!" she said.

Elizabeth and Todd began running toward them with a man and a woman in zoo uniforms. As soon as they reached the pipe, the two zoo workers knelt down and coaxed the

51

chimp all the way out of the pipe with another banana. In a moment, the woman was
holding the runaway chimp in her arms.

The rescue mission was over.

CHAPTER 8

Reunion!

"You did a wonderful job," the woman said to Jessica and Winston. "Thank you."

Jessica was smiling from ear to ear. She looked at her sister. Elizabeth was grinning just as hard.

"It was simple," Winston was saying. "I decided to use my banana—"

"*You* decided?" Jessica interrupted, glaring at Winston.

Winston scuffed his feet on the ground. "Well, it was really Jessica's idea," he mumbled. "And she found the chimp first, too."

"Thank you, Jessica," the woman said. She hugged the chimp tightly. "We've been pretty worried about this little one. Let's take her home now."

The two adults, four children, and one chimpanzee went back down the path toward the monkey house. "Did you get to pet her?" Elizabeth asked Jessica.

Jessica shook her head. "No, but I almost did."

"Did you really think of using the banana to get her out?" Elizabeth asked.

There was no time for Jessica to answer. As the group turned the corner, they saw Mrs. Wakefield, Mrs. Becker, and the whole class outside the monkey house. They looked like they were doing nothing but waiting for Elizabeth, Jessica, Todd, and Winston.

"Uh-oh," Todd said.

Jessica's stomach flip-flopped when she saw her mother. Suddenly, she felt relieved and happy and very, very sorry for sneaking off on purpose.

Their classmates surrounded the foursome and began asking questions.

"Did you all get trapped in the gorilla cage?" Ken Matthews shouted.

"Weren't you scared to be lost?" Ellen Riteman asked.

"Did you catch the chimp all by yourselves?" Jerry McAllister wanted to know.

Jessica looked around at everyone who was asking her questions. It was fun to be the center of attention! But she didn't know which question to answer first.

Luckily, the zoo worker answered for her. "Thanks to these four students, and especially Jessica, our little chimp is now safe and sound," she announced. "The zoo is very happy they helped us out. And if you can wait a few minutes," she added, "we'll give you a special tour of the monkey house."

"Hooray!" everyone yelled.

Everyone gathered around the chimp to look at her. But Mrs. Becker pulled Jessica, Elizabeth, Todd, and Winston to one side. Mrs. Wakefield listened silently, but she had a very serious expression on her face.

"I'd like to talk to you four," Mrs. Becker said. They all nodded, and Winston gulped loud enough for them to hear.

"We've been very worried about you," Mrs. Becker said. "Did you get lost, or did you just decide to go off by yourselves?"

Jessica looked at her sister. For a long time, no one said anything. Then Jessica

slowly raised her hand. "It's my fault," she whispered. "I made them come with me."

"You understand that it was very wrong, don't you?" Mrs. Becker asked. "Even though you found the chimp, it was wrong to leave the group."

All four looked at the ground. Jessica thought she was going to cry.

"We're sorry," Elizabeth said. Jessica and the boys nodded their agreement.

"We know you are. And we know you won't do it again. Now let's go see the monkeys," Mrs. Becker said.

As the rest of the group filed into the monkey house, Mrs. Wakefield held Jessica and Elizabeth back. She was so quiet while she looked at them that Jessica began to feel nervous.

"I'm very, *very* angry with you both," their mother said. "You scared me by getting lost."

"I'm sorry, Mommy," Jessica said. This time she wasn't upset about being scolded because she knew she deserved it.

Mrs. Wakefield smiled slowly. "But I'm also proud of you for rescuing that baby chimp." She hugged them both. "But don't you *ever* do anything like this again!"

"We won't, Mom," Jessica said. "Ever, ever again. I promise." She crossed her heart and snapped her fingers twice, and so did Elizabeth. It was their secret promise sign.

Mrs. Wakefield hugged them each again. "OK. Now let's go see your chimp."

She took each girl by the hand and they went into the monkey house.

CHAPTER 9

Inside the Monkey House

The woman in the zoo uniform said her name was Miss Weatherby and she was in charge of the monkey house. "We keep it dark inside so that the animals can't see us. We can see them, though."

Behind large glass windows were bright, lighted rooms for the monkeys. They barely looked like cages.

Miss Weatherby led the group to one window. "Who knows about monkeys and apes?" she asked.

Andy Franklin raised his hand. "I do. An

ape is a gorilla or a chimpanzee." Andy knew a lot about everything.

"Or an orangutan," Amy Sutton chimed in. She knew a lot about animals. "Right?"

Miss Weatherby nodded. "Right. Monkeys have tails and apes don't. That's the easiest way to tell them apart. Let's take a look."

Elizabeth nudged Jessica with her elbow. "Aren't you glad we get to see the monkey house after all?" she said.

"Y-E-S," Jessica spelled out. She didn't look upset anymore. She looked happy and excited.

Elizabeth was proud that her sister had found the chimpanzee. And it was all because of Jessica that they got to see the monkeys and apes.

"Now," said Miss Weatherby. She stopped in front of another cage. Inside, small monkeys were chasing each other around on a jungle gym and swinging by their tails. "Are these monkeys or apes?"

"Monkeys!" everyone shouted. "They have tails!"

Elizabeth and Jessica and almost everyone else started laughing. The little monkeys ran so fast they bounced off the walls! It looked like a fun game of tag.

"These are squirrel monkeys," Miss Weatherby explained. "Now let's take a look over here."

Behind the next window was a huge room full of chimpanzees. While they watched, a door in the back opened, and the runaway chimp came in. A large chimpanzee in the corner walked over and picked her up.

"Is that her mother?" Jessica called out.

"Right," Miss Weatherby answered. "Doesn't she look happy to have her little girl back?"

Elizabeth took her own mother's hand and squeezed it. Mrs. Wakefield leaned down to kiss the top of her head. "I'm glad to have *my* two girls back," she said with a chuckle.

Miss Weatherby showed them all of the apes and monkeys, and told them interesting facts about each kind. Elizabeth couldn't decide which ones she liked best. Finally, she decided she liked them all.

Two other people in zoo uniforms came and spoke to Miss Weatherby for a moment.

"I want to make an announcement," Miss Weatherby said. She led the way back to the chimpanzees. "The little chimp who got lost today is only four months old, and she didn't have a name until today."

"You mean you're going to give her a name right now?" Lila Fowler asked.

Miss Weatherby nodded. "Yes, we have the

perfect name for her." She looked over at Jessica and Elizabeth. "We're going to call her Jessica."

There was silence for a moment. Then everyone burst out laughing.

"You're naming the chimp after *me*?" Jessica gasped. Her eyes looked huge.

"That's right. Unless you don't want us to," Miss Weatherby said.

"I do!" Jessica shouted. "I do! I do! I do!"

Everyone looked in at the chimpanzees. Little Jessica was asleep in her mother's arms. Elizabeth was so proud of her sister she wanted to jump up and down.

"This is the best trip to the zoo ever," Elizabeth said. "Isn't it, Jess?"

Jessica nodded. "It sure is."

CHAPTER 10

Lost and Found

Jessica was still the center of attention during lunch. First Lila and Ellen and Caroline argued with each other about who would get to sit next to her. Then Caroline told Jessica she could use her brand-new eraser that was shaped like a strawberry. Lila told Jessica she could borrow her Madame Christina doll.

Jessica decided to sit in between Elizabeth and Mrs. Wakefield. "I'm really glad you're the class mother for this trip, Mom," she said, munching her peanut butter sandwich.

Mrs. Wakefield smiled. "Thank you, honey. I'm glad you said that."

"Except there's only one thing wrong," Jessica went on.

"What's that?" her mother asked.

Jessica looked at her sister, and Elizabeth made a sad face. Elizabeth knew what the bad news was.

"I lost my bracelet," Jessica said in a low voice. She held up her bare arm. "See?"

Mrs. Wakefield shook her head and made a "tsk-tsk" sound. "I'm so sorry, Jessica."

"And we looked everywhere!" Jessica added. "That's how I found the chimpanzee. And that's why we were gone so long."

Mrs. Wakefield took a sip of her apple juice. "Well, why don't we stop by the zoo office before we leave. Maybe someone found it and turned it in."

Jessica bounced up and down at her seat. "Good! I sure hope so."

After lunch, Mrs. Becker's class stopped at the souvenir shop. Elizabeth chose a postcard of a lion cub and a pen with a monkey that went up and down a tree. Jessica couldn't decide between a hat that said "Please Don't Feed This Animal!" and a sticker with peacocks, parrots, and other colorful birds on it.

"The sticker is prettier, but the hat is funnier," Elizabeth said. "Just go eeny-meeny-miney-mo."

Jessica shrugged. "OK." She counted off silently, and landed on the sticker. She frowned. "I want the hat though," she said.

When everyone had bought what they wanted, it was time to leave and get back on the bus. But Jessica, Elizabeth, and Mrs. Wakefield went to the main office first.

"Did anybody turn in a bracelet?" Jessica asked hopefully.

The man behind the desk raised his eyebrows. "What kind of a bracelet? I can't give anything back unless you describe it accurately."

Jessica looked up at her mother and smiled. "That's easy. It has beads and says my name on it. *Jessica.*"

"Well . . . let me just take a look here." The man opened a drawer and searched through it. "No, no, no," he muttered. Then he lifted one finger. "Aha!" He pulled something out of the drawer.

"My bracelet!" Jessica shouted. "Hooray!" She took the bracelet from him.

"Thank you," Mrs. Wakefield said to the man. Then she held out her hand. "Why don't you let me keep it until we get the clasp fixed?"

Jessica handed the bracelet to her mother. "I'm so happy we found it."

To Jessica's surprise, Elizabeth started to giggle when they left the office. "Look," she said. "That describes our whole day."

Jessica looked where her sister was pointing, and she started to giggle, too. There was a sign with large red letters.

"*Lost and Found,*" Jessica read aloud. "That's us!"

On the bus ride home, Lila and Ellen sat next to the twins.

"You'll never guess what we heard," said Lila.

"Yes," Ellen said. "We're the only ones who know. We weren't supposed to hear."

Jessica and Elizabeth looked at each other. They both knew how much Lila liked to re-

peat what other people said. Especially if it was a secret.

"Well, are you going to tell us?" Jessica finally asked.

Lila smiled. "Mrs. Becker is getting married again."

"What?" Elizabeth and Jessica both said together.

"It's true," Ellen said. "Mrs. Becker was talking to Lila's mother and—"

"She's marrying someone from Sweet Valley," Lila interrupted. "I'm going to find out who it is."

Elizabeth sighed. She knew that Mrs. Becker's husband had died. And she was very happy for the teacher. "It's great that Mrs. Becker's getting married again, but I wonder if she'll still be our teacher," she said.

"You're right," Jessica said. "Maybe Mrs.

Becker will go on her honeymoon and never come back."

The four girls looked at one another in alarm. They thought Mrs. Becker was a wonderful teacher.

"We can't let that happen," Jessica said.

Will Mrs. Becker get married and never return? Find out in Sweet Valley Kids #9, ELIZABETH'S SUPER-SELLING LEMONADE.

SWEET VALLEY TWINS

Buy them at your local bookstore or use this handy page for ordering:

Bantam Books, Dept. SVT3, 414 East Golf Road, Des Plaines, IL 60016

Please send me the items I have checked above. I am enclosing $_____
(please add $2.50 to cover postage and handling). Send check or money
order, no cash or C.O.D.s please.

Mr/Ms _____

Address _____

City/State_____ Zip _____

SVT3-7/91

Please allow four to six weeks for delivery.
Prices and availability subject to change without notice.

SWEET VALLEY TWINS™

Join Jessica and Elizabeth for
big adventure in exciting
SWEET VALLEY TWINS SUPER EDITIONS
and SWEET VALLEY TWINS CHILLERS.

☐ #1: CLASS TRIP   15588-1/$2.95

☐ #2: HOLIDAY MISCHIEF   15641-1/$2.95

☐ #3: THE BIG CAMP SECRET   15707-8/$2.95

☐ SWEET VALLEY TWINS SUPER SUMMER
FUN BOOK by Laurie Pascal Wenk
                         15816-3/$3.50/3.95

Elizabeth shares her favorite summer projects &
Jessica gives you pointers on parties. Plus:
fashion tips, space to record your favorite
summer activities, quizzes, puzzles, a summer
calendar, photo album, scrapbook, address book
& more!

CHILLERS

☐ #1: THE CHRISTMAS GHOST   15767-1/$3.50

☐ #2: THE GHOST IN THE GRAVEYARD
                         15801-5/$3.50

☐ #3: THE CARNIVAL GHOST   15859-7/$2.95

- -